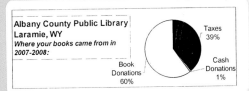

Thanks to my mom, and also Yuko and Marcos.

Library of Congress Control Number: 2007936992
ISBN-10: 0-439-63408-3
ISBN-13: 978-0-439-63408-3

10 9 8 7 6 5 4 3 2 1    08 09 10 11 12 13

Printed in Singapore 46
First edition, March 2009
The illustrations were done
in ink and Photoshop.
Book design by
Lillie Mear and
Sara Varon

# CHICKEN AND CAT CLEAN UP

## BY SARA VARON

SCHOLASTIC PRESS    NEW YORK

CHOMP!

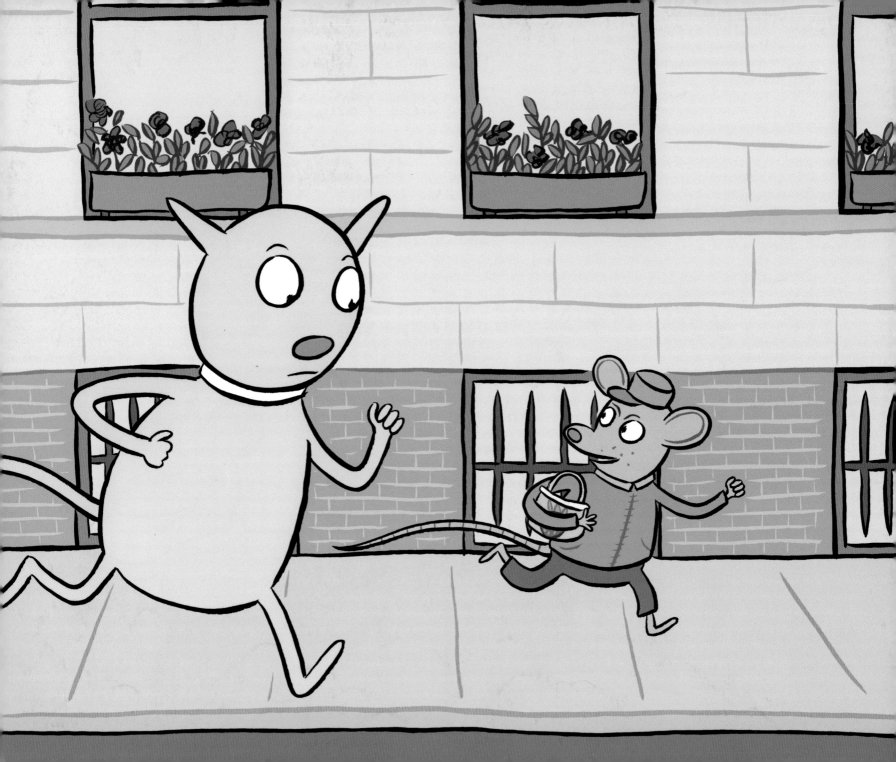

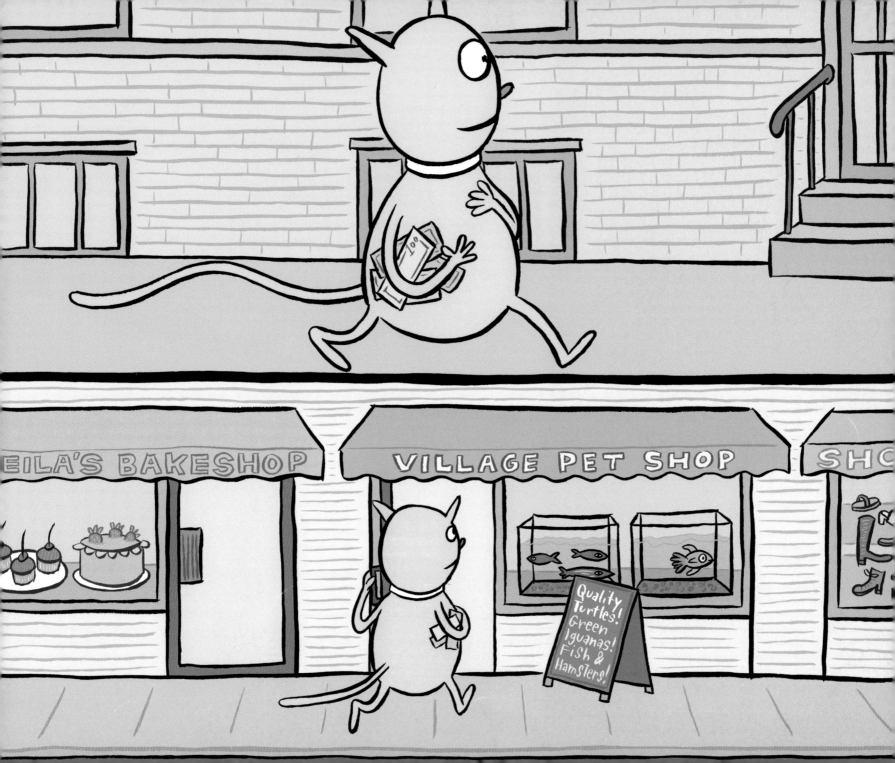

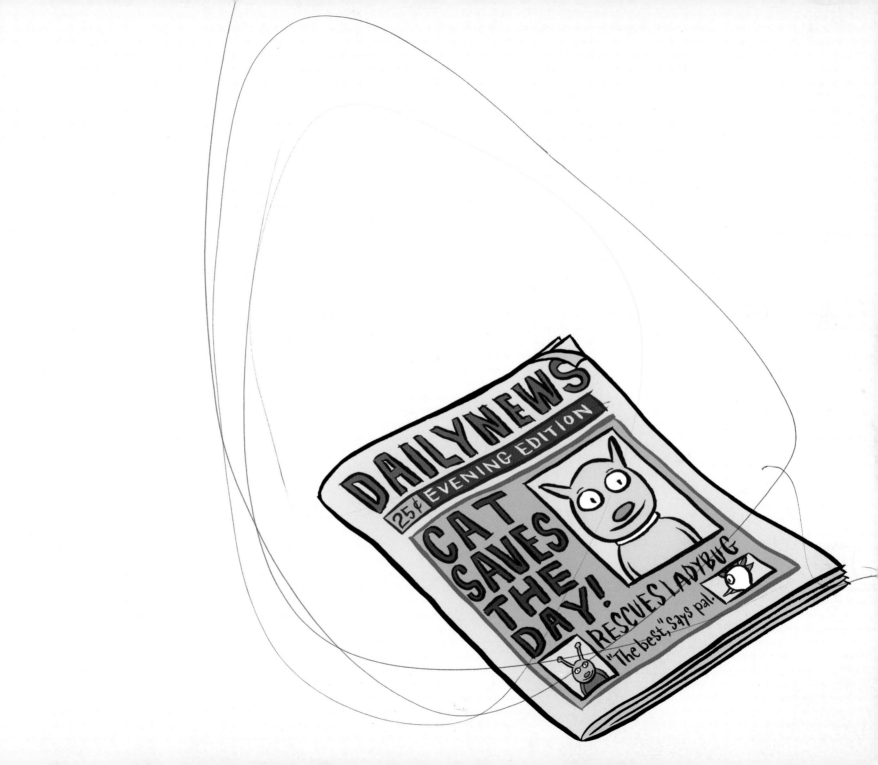